ALIEN TRANSACTION

JULIET CARDIN

This is a work of fiction. Names, characters, places, and incidents are products of the author's imagination or are used fictitiously and are not to be construed as real. Any resemblance to actual events, locations, organizations, or persons, living or dead, is entirely coincidental.

World Castle Publishing, LLC
Pensacola, Florida

Paperback ISBN: 9798891260023
eBook ISBN: 9798891260030
First Edition World Castle Publishing, LLC, July 3, 2023
http://www.worldcastlepublishing.com

Cover: Karen Fuller
Editor: Karen Fuller

Chapter 1

You know how you hear of making a deal with the Devil, and it always turns out terrible? Years of watching *Supernatural* should have forewarned me never to do it. Not that I did do it. I was smarter than that. Satan always wants your soul in exchange for making your dreams come true. I did want the 'dream come true' part, but I wasn't willing to give up my soul. My body, however, was a different story.

I wanted something really bad—bad enough to make me consider making a deal with the King of Hell himself. Or at least someone just as bad. An alien, to be exact.

For years, I'd struggled to be an actress. A *famous movie* actress. I studied lines and auditioned my heart out, only to be told 'no' time and again. The more I got rejected, the more determined I was to succeed. Casting directors, producers, not to mention numerous agents, kicked me to the curb. 'Not quite right for us,' 'Too tall/short/thin/curvy,' 'Thanks but no thanks,' or just outright 'No way.' met me on a daily basis. Until one day when I stumbled upon a website promising to make my dream a reality. Any dream, really. I didn't have to order stuff or kill anything to make it happen. There were some rhyming words to say, but not until after the ritual was performed.

The moon had to be full or as close to being full as possible. Grass had to be beneath me, and I had to stand on something metal, which in turn rested on the grass. In one hand, I had to hold some kind of working electrical device such as a radio, a cellphone, camera, iPad, iPod, or whatever. In the other hand, a clump of earth.

So three years ago, I stood on the lid of my trashcan in my backyard, like a human lightning rod, praying it wouldn't rain. It was late at night, and the moon was high. It was summertime, so the air was warm. My neighbors were in bed, and I'd turned out all the lights in my tiny rented house. My spell stuff was ready on the porch or on the counter in my kitchen by the back door. I'd gathered it up and slunk like a thief into my own yard.

For ten minutes, I stood there and waited, just as the website instructed. Then, when I felt a tiny wave of friction in the palm of my hand from the little radio, I said the words I'd memorized.

"I call to the heavens, the stars, and sky,

Come forth to me, hear my cry.

Bring to me my heart's desire.

Grant my wish, set it afire."

And, as promised on the website, a static voice emitted from the radio. Eerily, it whispered, "What is it you wish?"

"To be a famous movie actress," I whispered back.

"What shall you offer in exchange?"

"My body." It's what the website had specified. What it actually meant was another matter.

Swirling bits of light began to generate before me, sparkling and dancing in the slight breeze. I was prepared, yet a little freaked out, as it began to form into the shape of a being. Soon, it gained more substance, although

I could still see through it.

Being the same height as me, I focused easily on the grainy, black eyes. The being's head was bulbous, large, and barely supported by a scrawny neck. Its body was grayish in color and narrow in the limbs, lending truth to the many depictions I'd seen paraded on television and in movies. It appeared strangely fragile. How could it be possible for these things to steal humans and whisk them aboard their ships, performing untold experiments on them? It must be their superior technology, I decided.

I watched in anticipation as the being's tiny mouth, lacking lips, opened a fraction, and I caught a glimpse of a pointy, pink tongue. Lowering my gaze to the apex of its thighs, I could detect no sex organs—it wore no clothing of any kind. *Are you male or female? Or both?*

"You will give your body?" the

alien asked.

I snapped my lingering gaze upward and felt a blush heat my cheeks. "Yes."

Being a famous actress would be worth a few anal probes. I had to keep the bigger picture in mind—getting what I wanted. How bad could it be? The website had specifically stated that these aliens were friendly and merely wanted willing bodies to study.

But then, another thought entered my mind. "Um, how long?"

"Three years," replied the alien.

"You probe me for three years?" *Oh, hell no.*

"Come back for you in three years," it clarified.

That didn't give me a lot of time to enjoy my success. "How long will you want me?"

"Wonnitte," it replied.

One night! I breathed a sigh of relief. "Then I'm free to get on with my life again?"

The alien nodded in affirmation.

I didn't need long to think it over. After all, the way things were going so far, I'd be lucky to catch any sort of break before that time. "Okay then. Deal."

The alien waved around its skinny arms with strangely large hands on the ends, looking like an excited Mickey Mouse. It reached out and took the radio from me, turning it this way and that, nodding its head, seeming to confirm something. And then its body began to turn transparent and was about to vanish, taking my radio along with it. But I needed more information.

"Wait! How will you find me?" There was no way I planned to live an enchanted life in this dump. Sure, I was in Los Angeles, but far from the glitz and glamour where I envisioned myself.

The alien became more solid again. Waving its hand over the radio, I saw my fingerprints suddenly light up. "I find," it assured me.

I gulped and nodded. Then it faded away. The last things to vanish were its big, black eyes and a sinister little smile.

I shivered but felt a wave of satisfaction. Like it or not, I was about to get my wish. Besides, I assured myself as I gathered up my stuff and hurried back inside. How bad could one night possibly be? Afterward, I'd be free to return to my life of fame and fortune. I could hardly wait.

Chapter 2

Oh, what a fool I was. A poor, trusting, pathetic fool! For three days now, I'd sat in a small caged cell, barely room enough to stand or stretch or lie down. My beautiful, expensive clothes had been swapped for a short, one-piece, sleeveless tunic like a cave girl would wear. My feet were bare. My costly shoes were taken, and I received nothing in return.

It appeared that I was in some kind of cargo hold, on a spaceship of some sort, flying through the universe to God knew where. All around me were other cells, filled with all sorts of duped losers just like me. Some of them weren't even human.

Exactly three years to the day of making that cursed deal, the alien returned to collect his due. I'd been strolling the acres of lush gardens around my grand, beautiful home in Beverly Hills, basking in my success with a gorgeous hunk, when all of a sudden, my companion froze. The air had crackled with static electricity, and I'd been shocked and caught unawares as tiny glowing particles began spinning around before me and soon formed into the little bugger.

"Damn! Is it that time already?" I'd demanded, desperate for a way to escape.

The alien had nodded its bulging head and reached for me with greedy hands. Before I could do or say anything,

I'd begun to feel funny, and everything became blurry. My body disintegrated into thousands of pulsing atoms right before my eyes. And then I was swirling and whirling upward, farther and farther from my life on Earth.

Soon, darkness surrounded me, except for the multitude of twinkling stars. Beside me, the alien's particles guided my bits through the blackness. Though not able to see through my eyes as I had done in my body, I was somehow acutely aware of everything around me, as though all my senses were magnified and finely tuned. Before us, I had 'seen' a giant ship resting among the stars, and when I 'gazed' back, I saw a giant blue and white ball that I soon realized was Earth.

Our glowing pieces passed right through the spaceship, and then I felt myself becoming whole again. As I returned to body form, I staggered and fell to my knees. The alien beside me, now whole as well, seemed unaffected when I peered up at it. While I was dazed, it ushered me off toward a giant room filled with crates and large cages. And this was where I'd remained ever since.

Twice daily, a one-eyed hunchback brought me food and cleaned out my slop bucket. I was reduced from living a life of grandeur in a mansion on two acres of land, with five bedrooms, six bathrooms, and my own gourmet cook, to eating what resembled warm barf on a tray and crapping in a bucket. Where did I go wrong?

As soon as the alien tossed my stumbling form into the cage and shut the door, I'd reminded it not to take me too far. "You have one night. That's the deal."

"Wonnitte." This time the

pronunciation sounded different.

"Wait a sec. What are you saying?"

"Wonnitte, in human years...." It wiggled around those sausage fingers as though calculating. "Ten."

"Ten? Ten freaking years?"

It'd nodded.

"No. Oh no. No damn way! I'll be a dried-up old husk by then! Hollywood will forget all about me." I'd really only be thirty-five. In my prime, actually, but still, I wasn't kidding about my career being over. Not to mention my house and my car and all my furniture would be long repossessed by then.

The alien regarded me for a moment, then shrugged its bony shoulders. "Too bad."

As it waddled away, I screamed at it. "Scammer! Liar! You can't keep me for ten years." But it hadn't done any good, and I hadn't seen the alien since.

I spent three more days in that cage. The groans and cries around me made me want to scream in agony and denial. How could this be happening to me? Why hadn't I navigated the details of this deal more wisely? I'd been so quick to jump into a fantasy life that I'd neglected to check the fine print.

The cages around me contained mostly young women. Young, stupid women like me. Ones who'd been reckless or desperate enough to make lousy deals. When we'd managed to compare bits and pieces of our shared misfortune, we speculated our fate and poor choices. No one had any idea where we were headed or what would happen to us.

On the morning of what I guessed to be my seventh day of incarceration, I was finally allowed out of holding. The a-hole alien who'd been my undoing finally made an appearance and escorted me through the long, winding halls of the ship. Staring at the back of its big head as it waddled ahead of me down the narrow corridors, I knew it'd be dead on the spot if only looks could kill.

We entered a room that contained a large table and many chairs. Seated at the head of the table was a giant of a man who appeared to be human. Our gazes met and held as the alien pulled out two chairs, and we both sat down across from the giant.

I gulped as my eyes perused the man. His hair was short and blond. Bare arms covered with an array of tattoos and rippling with muscles rested on the table. Even though he was seated, I could tell he was tall. Probably well over six and a half feet. A black t-shirt and a black leather vest strained against his chest. Blue eyes, like a clear, bright sky, watched me intently. I suddenly felt self-conscious, sitting there wearing my smelly, short dress covered in sweat, and God knew what else. How I longed for an outfit, any outfit, from my mammoth walk-in closet.

"This is she?" the man asked in a deep voice that made me shiver.

"Yes," the alien replied. "Pretty. From Earth, as you…request."

Though they both had a strange alien lilt to their voices, at least I could understand what they said. My eyes scanned the room, desperate for an escape route. The only door I could detect was directly behind me. The windows I faced were long and wide, offering up breathtaking views of outer space. Stars and planets whirled by at an alarming pace, which seemed strange, considering the floor beneath me was steady and still.

If I made a run for it, I could probably bolt into the hall. But then what? I refused to accept the fact I was out of options. Somehow, someway, I must make an attempt to flee; otherwise, I'd never forgive myself.

Just as I was about to make my move, the giant reached into his vest and pulled out a small sack. Intrigued, I watched as he pushed it across the table, and the alien took it. I wondered how it was going to open it with those hands, but it managed to tug the string a smidgen and then proceeded to dump the contents out. I saw an assortment of colorful crystals that seemed to pulse with light.

"So we have a deal?" the giant asked.

The alien nodded.

"A deal? What deal?"

Both of them ignored me.

The giant rose to his full height. *Closer to seven feet.* He strode down the length of the table and came up behind my chair. "Let's go."

I twisted my head, staring at him until understanding dawned on me. "Wait. You're selling me?" I looked at the alien for some sign of refusal, but it was intently pawing its gems.

"Come," the giant said, his voice deep and unrelenting.

What choice did I have but to get to my feet? The giant put his hand on my arm and led me from the room. The alien never once even turned to see the look of confusion and despair I knew I wore on my face. My presence, it seemed, was inconsequential. It had bartered me away without a single thought or care, as though I were a pretty trinket, easily replaced. But then again, he had a cargo hold full of pretty trinkets. I could only hope and pray that my fate would be kinder than theirs.

Chapter 3

"There must be some mistake," I insisted as I was ushered at a near jog back down the hallway.

My companion remained silent, seeming intent to get to wherever he headed in a hurry. We pushed through a door and entered what appeared to be a landing bay. Several small ships encompassed the space, along with a short landing strip that ended at huge double doors.

We stopped before one of the ships, and the giant fiddled with a remote he'd fished out of his vest. A doorway lifted up from the side of the ship like a giant wing, and a row of stairs shot out. Still holding tight to my arm, he escorted me up into the belly of the beast. By the time I turned around to argue, the stairs had disappeared, and the large door came down, locking us inside.

The interior of the ship was well-lit, allowing me to see around. It looked similar to a small airplane but with a wider belly. At the front end were two bucket seats set before a vast control panel. Two more seats were set on either side of the back section. We were the only ones on board. The giant led me toward the front of the ship, sat me down, and strapped me into one of the chairs. He took the other one.

"Wait a sec," I said as he turned his attention to the controls. "Where are you taking me?" Dozens of scenarios played out in my frantic mind, none of them good.

"Let me get us out of here, then we'll talk."

He worked the control panel, flipping and switching stuff, and I watched out the front window as the ship rumbled to life and began taxiing over to the runway, slowly gaining momentum. The double doors opened up, and we surged forward, zooming out into space in seconds.

My head felt molded to the seat. With effort, I compelled my body forward, trying to fight against the force. "S-slow down."

"In a second," he said, gritting his teeth, his features straining.

Finally, he eased up on the control arm, and our speed leveled off to something sane.

I glared at him from my seat, gently

prying my clawed hands from the arm of my chair. "Why the rush?"

"I don't trust those bastards," he announced, becoming preoccupied with viewing the monitor and seeing what was going on behind us. A few moments later, he wrinkled his nose and turned his gaze on me. "Gad, you're ripe."

"Oh, a real gentleman you are," I fumed, embarrassed. "Let's see how good you smell after a week in a cage, shitting in a bucket." It was sad but true.

"That good, huh?"

His smile thawed my icy veins. I smiled back at him tightly, not completely forgiving him for his rudeness. "Who are you?"

He stuck out his hand, which I shook. It was firm and warm. "Gator. And you?"

I raised an eyebrow but refrained from commenting on his name. "Flora.

Flora Dale," I stressed, wondering if he'd heard of me. When he remained silent, I said, "Thanks for rescuing me."

"Rescuing you?"

"You did rescue me. Didn't you?" *Oh great.* The fidgeting thing he did for a few moments while refusing to meet my gaze worried me. I closed my eyes and sighed. At least this was better than the alternative. So far. "So, what are your plans?" Even from where I sat, I could see the hard bulge in his tight leather pants. Sex then?

"I, uh, needed a trade."

"A trade? As in, you traded for me so you could use me to trade for something else?" I tried to control my rising panic.

"Yes." He still wouldn't meet my gaze.

"What is it you want?" My mind worked frantically. Maybe there was something I could offer in exchange.

He stared at me grimly then, no doubt reading my thoughts. "Something you can't supply."

"Don't be too sure."

He looked away. "I am sure. My woman, Mila, was taken from me. In order to get her back, I must offer up an exchange."

Meaning me. "You must love her very much." *Despite the fact you referred to her as 'your woman,' as though you're a Neanderthal.* I was doomed.

"Love? Yeah, I need her."

I shook my head. "Need isn't the same as love. If you're willing to swap me so coldheartedly, then she must mean the world to you." I could see how he came by his name.

"She does." He stole a quick glance at me. "If you consider it coldhearted, then so be it. You Earth women are so complicated. That's why I—"

"Why you what?"

"Nothing." The grim look on his face told me I'd get no explanation.

We sat in silence for a while. The view from his ship was spectacular. I hadn't been able to see anything while aboard that big ship, being locked away as I was, except for those brief glimpses in the last few minutes. The blackness of space was vast, appearing endless. We passed huge planets and zigzagged around asteroids.

As the miles flew by, my curiosity got the better of me. "Where are we going?"

"A planet named Balenzie. It's a cold, barren, ruthless planet, home to thieves and cutthroats. The gang that took Mila is holed up in caves there." He made them sound like a bunch of pirates.

"Couldn't you send in authorities?

You must have some kind of law and order out here?"

He shook his head. "We do. But they won't help."

"Why not? Is it because she's a woman?" I had to ask.

"No. It's a huge risk to go in and confront these guys. They're dangerous. The Pozart—authorities—refuse to risk it for…." He paused for a moment. "Mila isn't like other people. She's special. Very special. One of a kind, really."

"All the more reason for these Pozart guys to help you."

His hand flexed on the control stick, and he rolled his shoulders while squeezing his other hand tight. "They won't risk it to save a golem." His voice was barely a whisper.

"A what?"

"A golem, okay? She's not like me or you."

I couldn't believe what I was hearing. "Then what is she like? What the hell is a golem?"

"I've said enough."

I glared at him even though he refused to meet my gaze. "I think I have a right to know, considering you're willing to swap me for her."

"Fine," he snapped. "She's not real. I built her with my own two hands."

"She's a machine? A robot?"

Now, he did meet my eyes. The cold blue stare he gave me made me swallow hard. "She is much more than that."

I turned my gaze back toward the windshield, thinking it wise to keep my contempt to myself. Refusing to resort to tears, I had to swallow down the lump in my throat to ask, "How long 'til we're there?"

"I had to chase that damn ship you

were in for days, trying to contact them and reach a deal just to get them to let me come on board. It was no easy task. We have a long way to go."

Good. I needed all the time I could get to make him change his mind. All my years of acting school would be put to the test. Although, this time, I wasn't playing at make believe. I was playing for my life.

Chapter 4

Gator had to stop sometime. Even if he possessed the stamina to fly for several days and nights without taking a break, the ship still needed fuel. At least, I hoped it did. In the meantime, I filled the endless vacuum of darkness by talking. Anything and everything I could come up with, hoping to thaw Gator's block of ice heart. I'd heard somewhere that talking to your abductor and getting them to relate to you was the first step in getting out of a messy situation.

Granted, Gator wasn't actually my

captor, but he was about to do something bad to me by handing me over to some brutal thugs. I had to get him to see me as a person. Someone who had the right to safety and survival, just as any person had. Mila, on the other hand, did not have wants and needs of any sort. Not when she was a machine. Gator needed to come to this realization by whatever means necessary.

After talking about myself for hours, I finally asked, "What's Mila like?" Maybe by his own admission, he would come to the conclusion of just how different she and I were. That what he planned to do to another living, breathing, feeling individual was wrong on so many levels, even if it meant being reunited with the love of his life.

His entire demeanor appeared to change. He visibly relaxed and eased up his vise grip on the control arm. Plus, his face became all dreamy like, as though he envisioned Mila dancing naked before him. He rolled his neck from side to side, the tension leaving his body in loud cricks and cracks. "She's uncomplicated."

"Unlike a real-life woman, you mean? One who has hopes and dreams?" I didn't want to anger him, but he needed to see the comparison of fact and fiction. When he ignored my question, I asked, "What made you create her? Was it companionship?"

"I guess."

It wasn't that I was really interested in Mila. She was a machine, after all. Besides wanting him to realize that she was not in mortal danger, nor was she afraid, it was also a fishing expedition on my part to find out what Gator searched for in an ideal mate. I intended to emulate everything he wanted or needed, a role I was determined to excel at.

I stared at a giant boulder as we passed by, swearing we got so close I could reach out and touch it. Though it may have appeared that I was merely passing time and making small talk, I attempted to focus solely on his words. I tore my gaze from the window, not allowing myself to become distracted.

How could I phrase this without sounding judgmental? "Ah, is there a shortage of women on your planet? Or maybe you have a problem with real women?"

Frowning, he said, "There are women on my planet." He ignored my other question.

"Is it because you travel a lot? Or maybe you don't want a relationship? Have you ever had a relationship?"

I heard him exhale loudly, and when I gazed at him, his face was a little red. "I do travel. I've been to Earth several times. I like it there—lots of nature. I even acquired a cabin on a lake, and we go to it whenever we get the chance."

He meant him and the machine, golem—whatever.

"A couple of years ago, before I built Mila, I went to the cabin and was out for a hike. I met this real looker. Sweetheart too. We spent the entire Earth summer together. Then, just when I think things are going great, she dumps me. Says 'thanks for the summer romance,' or something like that."

"So she broke your heart?" I filed that little tidbit of information away to peruse at a later time.

"I guess. She wasn't the first, either. I went around with a couple of women on Gaxtes—my planet."

"No luck?" I guessed.

"One was all wrapped up in her career, and the other one was as clingy as

Earth's Saran Wrap. I don't know. Maybe I expect too much or too little."

"Hence, the creation of Mila." Did I have any right to judge him, considering how I'd bartered my body for success and wealth? We'd both gone about getting what we wanted in unorthodox methods, leading us to our present unfortunate circumstances.

"She's everything a man could want. Beautiful, sexy, smart, funny. Always in the mood."

My ears perked up at his revelation. I couldn't help but blurt, "You built a sex machine?"

His face turned red, and I couldn't tell if he was embarrassed or mad. "She's not a sex machine."

"But you just said—"

"Yes. She's fully functional in the sex department. She looks virtually real, feels real."

I stared at his large hands with those long, tapering fingers, imagining them crafting such a finely built machine as he described. "But she's not. You can't say that having her is like having a real woman," I insisted as gently as possible.

"Not exactly the same, but close. And I don't have the headache of arguments or jealousy, mood swings, or PMS—yes, I know *all about that.*"

"So you want a Stepford wife. Do you know all about *that*?" *Careful.*

"No."

"Well, rent the movie next time you're on Earth. Sounds like it'll be right up your alley."

"Up my what?" He raised an eyebrow.

"Forget it."

"Mood swings," he mumbled.

I attempted to tamp down my indignation and focused instead on what he'd said earlier. "You have an actual cabin on Earth?" According to him, he'd had nothing but bad luck in love while there—with real women, that was. Perhaps he'd be willing to change that?

"Yeah. Like I said, I like being around nature. We don't have a lot of it on Gaxtes. There used to be, a long time ago."

"I know what you mean. Over-industrialization. In the last one hundred years, Earth has changed so much."

"That's not the problem on Gaxtes. We're slowly sinking. Most of my planet was covered in ice, which was fine. We don't mind the cold. Now, everything's heating up and melting. The water level keeps rising, making people move closer and closer together. Many have searched elsewhere to relocate as the landmasses shrink and shrink. We're lucky we have the technology to leave the planet."

Wow, that was terrible. "How long does your world have?"

He shrugged. "Don't know for sure. Maybe a hundred of your years or so. Earth went through something similar over a billion years ago. We know eventually, the water will recede, and we can one day return home, maybe in a thousand Earth years. Not nearly as long as it took for Earth to become habitable."

"That's still a long time. So Earth's your backup plan, then?" I wondered how many aliens had already relocated to Earth. If they looked like Gator, they'd have no trouble fitting in. He appeared human enough, although I'd yet to see all of him.

"Seems that way. Unless I find somewhere else to go."

"And what about Mila? How do you think she's going to fit in on Earth?"

"Your world isn't quite ready for

her yet, I think."

"So, do you plan to hide her away in the woods? That's the only way it'd work. Unless you want a lot of unwanted attention."

His world's catastrophe could work in my favor if he'd only see reason. If I could convince him Mila wouldn't be a good choice as an Earth companion, I might actually be able to sway him in my direction. Of course, I'd have to do a lot of lying and simpering to pull it off, but if I could get him to take me home, I could eventually make a break for it.

He seemed to consider my words. "Yes. She would remain hidden."

His reasonableness didn't help me out any. I decided to try another tactic. "Seems a little lonely, don't you think? I mean, you can't take her out to dinner or dancing. You would even have to be careful going for a hike or a boat ride in case you run into anyone. She really wouldn't be a true companion."

"I know all that," he snapped.

Guess I struck a nerve. I decided to spell it out for him. "I'm only bringing it up because if you plan on living on Earth, then this is what your life will be like. Yes, you'll have Mila, but only Mila. If you make any friends, you can't exactly bring them home to meet her. How do you plan to live? Are you going to work? You'll have to unless you have an endless supply of money to live off of. And if you work, your co-workers will want to know about you. People get curious and ask questions."

"I don't know. Yes, I guess I'll need to work, but I can make a living at the cabin. I'm good with my hands. I can be an inventor or something. Nothing too high-tech, of course. Plus, I can grow food and hunt and fish. I'll only need to go to town maybe once a week at most."

"Looks like you have it all figured out," I said. He had an answer for everything. As much as I tried to poke holes in his plans, he filled them in just as quickly.

Out the window, I saw a huge planet looming ahead. Gator guided the craft in its direction, so I hoped he planned on stopping. As he maneuvered closer and told me to 'hold on' while the ship broke through the atmosphere, I became determined. If I couldn't convince him to forgo Mila for me, then I had every intention of getting free of him and somehow finding my way back to Earth, whatever it took. The alternative was too grim to imagine.

Chapter 5

Gator glided closer to the surface, which offered up views of large mountains and what appeared to be an endless desert; no lakes, ponds, or streams were detectable. There were several widely spaced domes, and I noticed the only vegetation came from inside them. A docking station was set up outside one of the domes, and when we landed, I figured we must be able to breathe the air. We disembarked, and I stood by while Gator gave instructions for his ship to workers at the station.

"We'll be back tomorrow early," he

ended off before turning to me. "Let's go. We'll head into the dome to eat and find someplace to sleep."

I kept my eyes open, taking in anything and everything. The short distance across the sand between the station and the dome was uncomfortably hot. Since a walkway had been built between the two, I figured the sand was too hot to walk on.

With every step I took, my spirits sank. My dress had already begun to stick to me, and I could feel droplets of sweat sneaking down my back and between my breasts. If I were to escape, there was no way I'd be able to duck out of the dome. Taking my chances in the open would be suicide. Even with a good supply of water, I lacked proper clothing, and my feet were bare.

Now, being on the ground, I could see the distance between each dome was far enough away that I could just barely make out the top of the closest one across the hot desert. I'd never make it on foot. Though the size of the area inside the dome we headed for was huge, like that of a small city on Earth, there was nowhere to run. Nowhere to hide.

We were delayed at the gates upon entry by two beefy guards. Gator had to state his business, which he said was for a rest and ship fuel-up along his journey home—a partial lie. The guards perused me briefly, but seeing my poor condition and that I was obviously being escorted, they disregarded me. I got the feeling that a lot of peculiarities passed in and out of these glass walls. There would be no help for me from them.

We were soon strolling down the narrow streets, looking for a place to spend the night. I might have stared at my surroundings in awe instead of speculation if it weren't for the fact that I was overwhelmed by what else fate had in store for me. I mean, how cool was it that I was actually walking around on an alien planet? If someone had asked me five years ago if I believed in alien life, I would have scoffed. Wouldn't nonbelievers be amazed that aliens not only existed but thrived throughout the galaxy and beyond?

Although, what I saw around me wasn't particularly extraterrestrial. The streets were narrow and cluttered with people and shops, just like back home—albeit the majority of offered items were something I couldn't fathom. Many of the aliens appeared the same as humans, except some who were oddly colored, shaped, or sported an extra eye or limb. Gator, of course, seemed oblivious to everything.

"Are we going to eat?"

We'd passed many restaurants with open patios where the food looked pretty weird and the patrons even weirder. The smells weren't bad, however, causing my belly to rumble, reminding me it'd been a while since I'd eaten anything substantial.

"Let's get settled first. Then I think we'll eat in the room. I've stayed here before. There's a half-decent inn close by."

"Afraid I'll scream for help if you take me out?" I teased.

He regarded me with amusement. "Scream all you want."

I took that as a bad sign.

Not much later, just as the dome began to glow with artificial light and the sky beyond grew dark and starry, we settled into a room at a three-floor walk-up inn. The room, which contained a queen-sized bed, a wide dresser, one huge window, a round table and two chairs, a funky entertainment unit I had no idea how to use, and an en suite bathroom, appeared clean enough.

"Who gets the bed?" I asked as Gator closed the door and began going through some papers on the dresser.

"It's big enough for both of us unless you want to sleep on the floor." He didn't notice my scowl. "I'm gonna order some food. You won't know what any of it is, but it'll be better than that slop they were feeding you."

I sat down on the bed, laid back, and closed my eyes, suddenly feeling exhausted. "How do you know what they fed us? You weren't there."

"Judging by the look of you, you're half-starved. You have time to shower before the food comes."

I opened one eye. "Is that a hint?"

"You kind of reek. Please bathe. Is

that better?" He fiddled with a square built-in on the wall. He pushed a button, and a voice sounded over it. I figured it was an intercom.

I got off the bed and stomped past him into the bathroom. After I stripped off my cavegirl tunic and spent about ten minutes figuring out how to work the toilet, I contemplated the glass stall I presumed to be the shower. I did manage to fill up a basin with water and what I hoped was liquid soap. I submerged my tunic into the warm suds and then went to the shower, but I couldn't figure out how to turn the damn thing on.

Surrendering, I wrapped a towel around my body that barely covered my boobs and bush. Leaning out the door, I called to Gator. "Can you help me in here? I can't work the shower."

He was speaking into the intercom thing and waved his hand at me to be quiet. He joined me in the bathroom a few minutes later.

"I was ordering food," he said. "We've got a bit of a wait."

"Sorry, but I can't figure this out."

His handsome lips curled into a smirk. Striking blue eyes became slits when they eyed my scantily clad form.

"See something you like?" I was being sarcastic. He'd already made it perfectly clear he found me foul, not to mention the fact he'd spurned real women for machinery.

Ignoring me, he adjusted the shower until a steady spray came out.

I reached around him to feel the temperature, my ample breasts pushing against his arm. "Too hot," I informed him.

He messed around a bit more. "Try that."

The fact wasn't lost on me that he

held his ground and waited for me to lean against him again. Or maybe it was my imagination, but I thought I heard a quick intake of breath. I watched him from the corner of my eye as I took overly long feeling the water, and I noticed he was staring at me. Not only that, but his body seemed quite tense all of a sudden. I stole a downward glance and noticed the bulge in his pants was quite substantial.

So now I had a couple of options running through my desperate mind. All of my talking hadn't seemed to make a dent in his armor. He appeared to bear no qualms about putting the fate of a robot over that of a human being. Maybe I could get through to him with a more hands-on approach. Perhaps then he wouldn't be so quick to swap me for Mila. I could try to seduce him, or I could accept my fate.

I let my towel drop to the floor.

"Oops," I gasped.

Instead of reaching for my towel, I leaped into the shower stall, which I gauged could easily accommodate the both of us—if he were so inclined. Now was the moment of truth. Would he take the bait, or would he simply walk away? I closed my eyes and allowed the spray of warm water to cascade over my short blonde hair and down my body. I bet Mila couldn't give him a show like this—not without short-circuiting or rusting out, that was.

"Ah, that feels so good," I said.

My finely tuned senses told me Gator hadn't left the room. I could hear his deep breaths and feel the heat of his stare.

"Is there soap?" I asked, fumbling around with my hands blindly.

Moments later, I felt a smooth bar slip into my palm.

"Thanks." I cracked open one eye while I lathered up my breasts. The soap had a subtle, pleasant scent. I made sure to soap every inch of myself in what I hoped was a slow and sensual manner.

I debated whether I should ask him to wash my back for me but decided more drastic measures may be required. I dropped the bar of soap. Making sure my back was to him, I bent over and began to search for it.

"Damn," I muttered for effect. "Can you see it? I don't want to open my eyes. I'll get soap in them."

"Yeah, I can see it," he ground out.

In the next moment, I felt a thick finger slide up inside my body. I squeaked and jumped, being caught off guard. Then, remembering my plan, I pushed aside any and all inhibitions and began to groan. Not wanting to stand and break the spell, I grabbed hold of my ankles and let the water rush over me, clearing away the rest of the suds. I groaned again when I felt another finger slide into my passage.

"Gator," I gasped.

"Flora, I—" he said at the same time.

"I want to," I assured him, sensing his hesitation.

After all, if this didn't work, I'd soon be facing a terrible fate.

Chapter 6

Gator pulled his fingers free while he struggled with his clothes. Soon, he had my hips gripped in his hands. The head of his erection nudged against me. I spread my legs wide as he began to push forward. The size of him surprised me. My passage stretched to accommodate and allow him to move deeper. Still, I groaned with the assault.

"You're so big!"

"I know."

Arrogant bastard. I was beginning to wonder if he'd built Mila because no ordinary female could contain him. Once he'd worked himself all the way inside me, he stopped. Seconds later, he began to move again. Slow strokes in and out. With every surge forward, each one grew harder and faster than the last, and I couldn't help but cry out. At first, uncomfortable, I soon became slicker and more turned on.

He thrust inside me for several minutes. Bent over, I began to feel lightheaded and giddy with excitement. I bent my knees and allowed him to support my weight with his hands. He held me tight, and I had no fear of falling, only of fainting.

When it seemed he would plunder me forever, I had to cry for mercy. "Please, I can't…take it."

He slowed his pace and slid his hands across my body to reach for my breasts. Gently, he lifted me upward so my back rested against his chest. In this position, I became even more aware of the great size of him.

With one arm wrapped around my waist and the other fondling my breasts, he began to have at me again. His hand on my belly moved down between my legs to play with my parts. My head rolled side to side against his chest, now wet from the spray of water. He lifted me to move us forward so we were both fully in the shower. Warm water rained down on us, washing away the slickness of sweat.

His hands tightened on my body suddenly, and his thrusts became even more eager. "This. Changes. Nothing," he ground out, each word accented by a thrust.

Sensing I was about to come, he stilled deep inside me, his fingers still playing as I cried out in pleasure. Waves of ecstasy rushed through me until my passion was exhausted. With my orgasm dimming, he began to stroke quickly once more until he froze, shouting out his own pleasure. I moved my hips while he came, all the while praying I'd been the best lay he'd ever had. Despite his words, I knew he'd enjoyed himself. Enough to keep me, I had no idea.

Having spent himself, he rinsed off and then moved onto the bathroom floor. He snatched my towel and laid it over the puddle we'd made, then he wrapped another towel around his hips in a poor attempt to conceal himself and left the room.

I rinsed off as well and turned off the spray of water, which took a full minute, despite having seen him work the controls. The only thing left to dry myself with was a hand towel, so I opted to air dry while I drained the basin and let cool water run over my dress. I wrung it out and hung it to dry over the high shower bar.

"Can I borrow a shirt?" I called out, leaning around the bathroom door. I was surprised to see Gator lying back on the bed, his head resting on his bent-up arms. The towel he'd used was laying across the bottom of the bed. His eyes were closed, and he appeared to be asleep.

Taking advantage of the opportunity, I tiptoed across to him and eased down onto the bed. I gazed at his body and marveled at the size of him. His member was hard and standing tall like a flagpole. I reached out and grasped it in my hand. He tensed a little, but his breaths remained even and deep. Wiggling closer to him, I bent down and licked the rim around the head of it. He seemed to grow even larger in my hand.

Seeing him up close made me

wonder how I'd ever fit him inside of me. Compared to his almost seven foot height and probably close to three hundred pounds of rippling muscle, I was just over five-foot-seven and about a hundred and fifty pounds. Not exactly model material compared to the six foot, hundred pound starlets I encountered in Hollywood.

Thinking about that life reminded me of how much I'd lost. The glamorous life I'd led was everything I'd hoped for…almost. Despite the fabulous roles I'd been given and living the life, I'd always dreamed about, I felt something lacking. There'd been endless parties at my swanky house and several invitations out. Many men filled my life, always hanging around, full of pretty words and lavish gifts, but it all seemed fake, like a made-up fairytale.

I guess when it came down to it, I

was lonely. There was no special someone in my life. No close friends, as I'd given up the few I'd had when I moved away. Caught up in the excitement, I'd lost contact with them and couldn't help but feel some regret. Making new friends was hard. I always wondered what inspired their interest; was it actually me, was it my bank account, or was it what I could do to further their careers? And the men who'd come into my life had disappeared just as quickly. I guess the thing I craved most was intimacy. Not just sexual, but companionship.

Remembering the deep sadness in Gator's eyes when he'd spoken of lost loves made me see a kindred spirit. He'd been so hurt and lonely that he'd been compelled to create a companion. I wondered what lengths I'd go to, given the opportunity, to fill the void in my own life. I felt slightly guilty that I wished to deprive him of his precious Mila. And yet, what about me and my life? I didn't deserve to be sacrificed this way.

Resolved, I decided to up the stakes. I had to show Gator that I was a flesh-and-blood woman, one to be reckoned with. I took his erection deep into my throat. With a squawk, he awoke and began to sit up. Through a haze of sleepiness, he noticeably realized he was being pleasured mercilessly. He threw back his head with a groan. I felt his fingers sink into my hair and tumble the damp strands. *Take that! Let's see your cherished machine blow you like this.*

Soon, having enough of my torture, he sat up and reached for me. Pushing me beneath him, he spread my legs wide with his knee. When I thought he'd plunge into me, he surprised me by kissing a trail down my body, ending up with his head between my thighs. His tongue laved at me for a while before he began suckling on my hard, little bud. My hips rose up in delight. I grasped the short strands of his hair and pulled him against me.

"Yes!" I cried out when I felt a thick finger sink into my passage, soon followed by another.

Taking mercy on me far too soon, he kissed his way up my body, taking special care with my hardened nipples, and came to rest between my legs. I felt the long, hard length of him against my thigh. When he lifted his head and stared into my eyes, I wanted to ask him what it was like going down on a machine, but I refrained.

He positioned himself before my entrance and surged forward, burying himself deep inside me. I arched my back and cried out with enjoyment. I was thrilled over the way our bodies moved together. Never before had a man demanded so much of me and given so much of himself in return. Gator kissed my lips, his tongue darting deep into my mouth, copying the movements of his penis. Strangely, I felt this was the most intimate gesture of all. When we both reached our peak together, he held me tight in his arms as he came deep inside me.

I stiffened as a sudden thought entered my mind. Caught up in the desperation of gaining his affection, I'd let myself become careless. What if a child was created? I knew there was a chance. I allowed myself to dwell on the thought for a moment or two. If a child was born of our union, then so be it. I might even plant the idea in Gator's mind, reminding him I could give him what Mila never could. Quite unexpectedly, a vision of us—Gator and I and our child—entered my mind, and a warm, gushy feeling rushed over me. Quite ridiculous, really, having only just met him. And yet, having a family of my own was a deep-seated fantasy I hadn't dared to shake off and examine in the past, but now I did.

When Gator opened his eyes, he saw the tears in mine.

"Did I hurt you?" The tender, concerned look on his face was endearing.

I shook my head. "No. It's just, I've never...." I didn't know how to explain what I'd felt.

"I know." He smiled at me, and I felt a connection forge between us.

When a knock at the door sounded, I squeaked and leapt to my feet to run and hide in the bathroom.

"That's our food," I heard Gator say.

A few minutes later, he called for me to come out. On the bed, he'd spread out several trays of food. I went in and sat down, feeling slightly self-conscious of my undressed state. Gator, oblivious to everything except the food in front of him, ignored my embarrassment.

Watching him, I had to wonder if I'd made any impression at all. The bond I'd felt earlier had all but dissipated. In the morning, would he declare he'd made a terrible mistake and take me home, or would he march me out to his ship, anxious to swap me for a robot?

Chapter 7

Gator and I spent the night in each other's arms. I felt warm and safe, sleeping the best I could remember in a very long time. In the middle of the night, we made sweet, sensuous love. I felt hopeful as I showered and dressed in the morning. When I left the bathroom, Gator was standing ready by the door.

"All set?" He kept his gaze diverted, and his tone of voice held no emotion.

A wave of panic threatened to send me to my knees. He wouldn't look me in the eye because he still planned on swapping me for Mila. That much was obvious. I wouldn't give him the satisfaction of seeing me cry or hearing me beg. I brushed past him and left our room. We didn't bother to stop and eat since it appeared neither of us had much of an appetite. Come to think of it, he'd acted aloof since we crawled out of bed at first light.

We strode through the city streets and exited the dome in silence. Frantically, I'd scanned the narrow lanes, silently pleading with anyone who'd meet my gaze to save me, but all I'd received were blank stares or suggestive leers.

Once aboard his ship, he flew off at a sedate pace. After flying for over an hour, he finally broke the silence.

"What did you think was going to happen? That I'd forget all about Mila?"

That's exactly what I'd thought. "I don't know."

"She's more to me than just sex."

I glared at him. "Unlike me, you mean."

"We talk and laugh. We get along. She listens to my hopes and dreams. She makes me feel good about myself, and I know she'll never leave me."

"'Cause it's all about you, isn't it?" Seeing the hurt on his face, I looked away. "Look, I'm glad she's all those things to you, but I'm having to pay a hefty price for your happiness."

"I'm sorry."

"Yeah, you should be. I didn't ask for any of this."

"So you have somewhere better to be?"

He didn't need to know how lonely I'd been on Earth. But before I could regale him with more stories about my glamorous life and wonderful, fulfilling career—false though it may be—he asked, "What were you doing on that alien ship?" His tone implied he already knew the answer.

"Is that why you targeted that particular ship? You figured we were doomed anyway, so it would justify what you had planned?"

"Maybe," he admitted. "There's rumors about those aliens, about how they experiment with humans and how they get them."

"So you know about the deals?" How embarrassing. It'd be one thing to claim abduction but quite another to admit I'd waltzed right into that mess, eyes wide open.

He shrugged. "Some."

I stared out the window. "If you must know, I made a deal to become a famous movie star for three years in exchange for being their guinea pig for what I thought would be one night. I was supposed to go back to being a star after that. Little did I know what their one night entailed."

He smiled. "Ah, wonnitte. They got you, did they?"

"Damn cheats."

We both contemplated the scenery for a while.

"So, this gang…what will they do to me?" I finally asked.

He had the decency to look guilty. "Not sure, really. They may sell you or play with you a bit…."

"Play with me?" I interrupted. "As in sex stuff or 'feed me my own limbs' stuff?"

"Not sure," he admitted.

The ship suddenly lurched violently to the right. If we hadn't been belted in, we would have gone flying.

"What the hell?" I demanded as we began to straighten out. As soon as the question left my mouth, we dropped drastically. "What's happening?" I cried.

Gator worked the controls like the Wizard of Oz behind the curtain. "Don't know."

"Do something!"

We began to spin out of control. I felt last night's dinner rise up in my belly. As soon as Gator steadied us for a few moments, something else would happen. The ship was completely out of control.

"There's a planet up ahead," he shouted. "Hold on. I'm gonna try and bring us in."

The planet looked bleak, all reddish and green tones mixed with lots of dark blue. Everything was swirling due to our wild approach. Time seemed to slow down. Fears bombarded me. Would we survive the impact? If we did, would the atmosphere be compatible to our bodies? How would we leave if the ship was damaged? Was the planet hostile? Would I ever see Earth again? And then I thought, *at least I won't die alone. I'm so glad I got laid before I faced death. Gator can't swap me now.*

"Here we go," he hollered.

We'd breached the atmosphere and were coming down hard and fast. The sight of trees gave me hope they'd cushion our landing and that there would be oxygen to breathe if we survived. Gator fought the controls, bringing us steady and pulling up the front end at the last second, so when we hit, the belly of the ship took the impact. We bumped, rattled, lurched, and squealed before finally coming to a rest. Both of us clutched our heads and groaned.

"Holy crap!" I cried.

Gator unbelted his restraints and wobbled to his feet. His hands came down on my shoulders, and he stared at me frantically. "Are you okay? Are you okay?"

"Stop yelling in my face. I heard you. I'm fine. I think."

He unbuckled me and pulled me into his arms. My head rested wearily on his heaving chest.

"Come on," he said, urging me toward the middle of the ship.

I saw that he meant to open the door, and I lunged for his arm. "Wait! The air could be poisonous out there."

He stared at me strangely. "Oh. Oh, yeah. You're right. Let me check it out." Leaving me standing there, he went back to the front of the ship. After doing something with the controls and staring out the window for several minutes, he called back, "It's okay. It's safe."

"What a relief." I waited while he returned to my side.

He opened the door, but before we

bailed out, he grabbed a duffle bag from a hidden compartment. Then he opened a few more compartments and began putting stuff into the bag. He fastened it shut and slung it over his shoulder. "We may have a hike ahead of us. Good thing I have supplies."

He jumped down, since the stairs appeared to not be working, and held out his hand to me. Once I was beside him, we began to walk the perimeter of the ship, assessing the damage. It looked relatively unscathed.

Gator grabbed a controller from his pocket and pushed a button to shut the door on the ship. "Let's head out," he said.

I regarded him for a moment. "Wait. Why?"

He stopped and turned to stare at me like I was a dolt. "What do you mean? We need to go for help. We can't stay here."

"The ship doesn't look that bad. Why can't you just fix it? I noticed a bunch of tools in those secret compartments you were going through."

He'd created Mila, so he was obviously skilled. Repairing his ship should be a walk in the park for him. I was surprised he was so quick to bail on it. But then, a glimmer of hope took root in my breast. Perhaps he wasn't in as much of a hurry as he claimed? Perhaps our night together had affected him more than he let on?

"Tools won't do me much good if I don't have the right parts," he replied.

Now I felt stupid, and that little spark of hope began to fizzle. "Okay. But if the controls worked well enough to check air safety, shouldn't they be okay for calling for help?"

What was the matter with me? Why

couldn't I just keep my big mouth shut? The perfect opportunity had presented itself to strengthen a bond between us. Dealing with a crisis made people reach out to one another, didn't it?

He glared at me. "Don't you think I thought of that? I sent out a distress signal while I was checking the atmosphere. No one answered."

"All right, all right, don't get all pissy. I'm just asking."

Relief washed over me, despite my words. Now we'd have our chance.

I graced him with a smile. "I'm sorry to be a nag. I'm just scared. I'm so glad you're with me to keep me safe."

I glanced around, making sure to set my features in wide-eyed fright. I saw his frown immediately turn into a smile of understanding.

He puffed out his chest at the thought of being my hero, making me duck my head to keep from snorting. "I'm pretty sure I know where we are. I believe this planet is named Taranus. If so, it's inhabited by an advanced alien race. It's also home to other species. We need to get out of the woods before nightfall," he informed me, swinging his gaze around to peer between the trees.

I inched closer to him. "That sounds ominous."

He began to walk, and smiling secretly, I trailed behind him. "There are beasts here more dangerous than those on Earth."

"Great." Now I was genuinely concerned. "Wouldn't it be safer in the ship then?"

"Yeah, until we run out of food and water." As he spoke, we passed by a little stream with purple and black fish that looked like salmon flopping around in it, but he ignored the sight.

I watched his back as he strode on determinedly. Broken branches and rocks scraped and scratched at my feet, but he didn't seem to notice or care. Whenever I hung back too far, he called to me to hurry up. He was in a rush, obviously. Yet I had the feeling it wasn't the threat of the wildlife that urged him on. No, he was anxious for us to be on our way again so that he could be rid of me and be reunited with his precious Mila.

Chapter 8

The forest appeared similar to Earth's. Although the trees were short and wide, the shape of the large, brightly colored leaves reminded me of dinosaur footprints. The trunks of the trees were almost black in contrast, their roots snaking out above ground, all around them like tentacles, making walking hazardous. The sky was deep blue, and I could see the outline of two small moons, enforcing the fact we were nowhere near my planet. The ground beneath my feet felt spongy. My feet made sucking sounds with almost every step I took, and when I lifted them up, little pools of water filled in the impressions I left behind.

Gator and I walked for what felt like hours, only stopping to pee or rest my aching feet. Having finally noticed my distress, he pulled a rag out from his bag and ripped it into strips, wrapping them around my feet to give me some relief.

The sky was darkening as we finally breached the forest. Standing with the trees at our back, I sighed in relief. The ground stretched out before us like a wave of red. Widely spaced trees dotted the landscape. Far off, around the outer edges of the area, I made out clusters of trees, also reddish in coloring—both the trunks and the leaves. Every surface, be it sand, stones, or tufts of grass, appeared to be colored in hues of red, and in the distance, I saw what looked like a small lake, judging by the crystal blue. My feet would appreciate this less treacherous terrain.

"This is pretty," I said. "I like how the ground is so smooth, then rises up into rippling hills, then back down into valleys. It's like looking at an ocean of red. Is that a lake?"

Gator nodded, seeming to be enjoying the view as well. "Yes. Now that we're out of the woods, you'll notice a lot of little lakes."

"What about scary beasts?" Scanning the area, I could see little bird-like creatures flying overhead and hear them twittering and chirping. A fluffy animal about the size of a rabbit jumped around in the trees, but it appeared harmless enough. Unlike in the forest, I didn't notice any widespread, large footprints. There'd been plenty of them behind us, making me wary over every step we took and every sound we heard. I hadn't wanted to catch a glimpse of the beast who left tracks like that behind.

"From what I've heard and remember, the larger animals prefer the forest, the smaller ones the hills and valleys. We should be safe here."

"Good. One less thing to worry about. So which way should we go? To find civilization, I mean."

He pointed straight ahead. "Not really sure, but let's try that way. We're bound to run into somebody soon." He began walking, and I followed along.

"Did you happen to hear if the inhabitants are friendly?"

He nodded. "For the most part."

Our pace became much slower, and instead of following Gator, I walked beside him. When I slowed even more, he matched my pace and swung an arm around my waist. I rested my head against him, liking the feel of his body beside mine, so tall and strong. It was hard to believe this man would dump me with a dangerous gang the first chance he got in exchange for a robotic sex toy.

Night soon arrived. The light cast from the moons was bright enough to guide our steps safely. We had walked a good distance when we, at last, came upon what resembled a miniature forest—certainly not large enough for giant beasts to inhabit.

I peered into the depth of the dark woods and gasped. "Is that a cabin?" As we got a few steps closer, my view became clearer. "Holy shit! That is a cabin."

We wound our way through the trees a short distance and soon stood before a small shelter sturdily built from logs. It was so quaint, I half-expected a fairytale witch to come skulking out and offer us candy.

Gator knocked on the door. When there was no answer, he tried the handle. To our surprise, it was unlocked. He bent his head into the interior and called out. Again, no answer and no guard animal had rushed out to attack us.

"Guess no one's home," he said.

As he moved to go inside, I caught his arm. "Wait, you can't just walk in."

He pulled free of my grip and entered anyway. I waited a bit, then followed him. It took a moment or two for my eyes to adjust.

"Over here." He'd gone in several steps and waited as I made my way over to him.

I latched onto the back of his pants and pulled up close to him. When the cabin remained quiet and calm, the frantic beat of my heart began to settle. Curiosity replaced my unease, and I took a look around. The interior was cozy, from what I could make out in the dim light. One entire wall was taken up by a stone fireplace, which had a neat stack of wood beside it. A table with four chairs tucked in around it sat in the center of the room. A large bed covered with a comforter was positioned into the corner of the opposite wall. The air was musty, and I had the feeling the place had been vacant for a while.

Gator slung the bag off his shoulder onto the table. Then he set to making a fire. He knelt before the hearth and put a couple of pieces of wood into it. Using a lighter he fished out of his pocket, he soon had bright flames giving off warmth and light. Getting to his feet and brushing off his hands, he went back to the table.

From the pack, he pulled out the food and water supplies. "Want to eat?" He sat down at the table while I stood restlessly where he'd left me.

"Do you think we should?" Seeing the look of exasperation on his face, I moved over to join him. "I feel like an intruder. What if whoever owns this place comes back?"

He had a mouth full of food, so I had to wait for him to answer. "No one's been here in a long time."

"So? They could come back, and I doubt they'd be impressed to see us making ourselves at home."

He shrugged. "If they ask us to leave, we will. In the meantime, I'd rather sleep in here than outside."

I shuffled from foot to foot, my poor feet hurting from our long walk, but I felt uncertain about sitting down. My stomach rumbled, so I reached for the canteen and took a long swig of water. Eventually, the pain and fatigue in my legs and feet won out, and I took a seat and started to eat, my nervous gaze darting between Gator and the door.

After a while, I began to relax. He was probably right when he said no one had been here for a long time. Maybe they would never return. I let my mind play out a little fantasy in which Gator decided to forgo his quest and, instead, declared his undying love for me. We decided to spend the rest of our days here, making love, living off the land, and going to bed each night wrapped in each other's arms. I let a sigh slip past my lips. It was a nice little dream. But looking up at him, shoving food into his mouth, a determined look on his face, I reminded myself that was all it was—a fantasy.

Exhaustion finally took precedence, and when he led me to the soft bed, I didn't object. I unwrapped my feet and took off my dress before settling in under the covers beside the wall. If anyone came in, they'd have to knock since Gator had locked and barred the door. Besides, they'd have to get past him before they got to me.

Gator stripped down and crawled in beside me. I felt his huge erection against my leg when I curled up against him. When he pulled me into his arms, I fell fast asleep.

****

The days passed easily nestled in the little cabin in the grove of trees. In spite of Gator's earlier rush to get to civilization and repair his ship so we could rescue Mila, he allowed us to settle into an easy routine. There'd been no objections from me.

He'd deemed the first few days as rest days, in which we made frantic love and gobbled up the remains of our supplies. Then he said we needed to restock our supplies before we could venture on, so he began to hunt and fish.

Once we were well stocked with food and water, he decided we should enjoy the fruits of his labors, so we fell back into the routine of indulging ourselves with food and sex.

I didn't have any regrets. The fact that he preferred to spend his time with me here, in this place, instead of rushing us on our way and eventually swapping me for Mila was a relief. I found myself catering to his every want and whim. Be it erotic sex, helping him fish, keeping him company while he chopped wood, or talking long into the night, I was up for it. For the first time in my life, I felt completely content. I longed to stay in this place with him forever—just like in my fantasy.

My life on Earth seemed a distant memory, one I was surprised to discover I didn't miss. Despite spending most of my years craving to be an actress, wasn't

I now playing the role of a lifetime? And as the days turned into weeks, I found I'd easily slipped into the play of Gator's life, his desires becoming my own.

One evening, about a month after our arrival, I was on my knees, pleasuring Gator's giant erection and cuddling his balls while he stood before the fire. His hands were buried in my hair, which had grown slightly longer.

He turned my head up to meet his gaze. "I love it here," he said, his tone wistful. "Flora, would you be opposed to staying on…indefinitely?"

I moved my lips from him and stared at him hopefully. "Really? Do you mean it?" I didn't want to break the spell, but I had to know. "What about Mila?"

He smiled. "You've come to mean so much to me. I couldn't imagine leaving you with those bastards. I don't know what I was thinking. I'm sorry."

I smiled back at him. "It's okay, I understand. You didn't know me then. And yes, I would love to stay here with you." I meant it too. My life on Earth, even with all the glitz and glamor, was a shallow comparison to what I had now with Gator. I'm not sure when it happened, but I'd fallen in love with him.

Gator turned me around, sank to his knees, and bent me forward so my rear end was high in the air. For several tantalizing minutes, he plunged into me without inhibition before he carried me to bed and finished us off. Soon we both fell asleep.

In the morning, I awoke before him, determined to make him a special breakfast to celebrate our life together. He'd discovered a sweet, apple-like fruit that grew not far off in the distance. He'd always insisted on going to get it alone, telling me I'd gobble up all the fruit like a little pig if he showed me where to find it, but I knew the general direction. Since he still lay asleep, he couldn't object.

As I strolled along, I smiled, feeling happier than I ever had in my life, even more so than when I'd enjoyed my dream career. This I'd achieved all on my own, with no wishes required. It'd taken several erotic-filled days and nights, but I'd finally proven to Gator that it was possible for him to have a great relationship with a real, live woman. I'd won.

Once I reached the orchard, I wandered deep into its depth, determined to find the plumpest fruit. I picked a piece of fruit and ate it while admiring the dark red blossoms on the trees. Tiny multi-colored insects buzzed around, along with colorful birds, adding to the surrounding beauty.

Suddenly, I came upon a giant pile

of brush that seemed out of place. Gazing at it, I suspected it wasn't naturally growing. When I tugged a branch free, I believed it to be camouflaging something. But what? Part of me wanted to leave it be, perhaps mention it to Gator, and together we could come back and investigate. The other part of me wanted to know what it was right now. I gave in to my impatient self.

After several minutes of pulling away the brush, I saw that it was a ship. Standing there staring at it, both sides of me battled for supremacy again. My idealistic side theorized that it had to belong to someone. Probably the person who owned the cabin. Perhaps they'd gone out hunting one day and hadn't returned? Maybe they'd met with foul play or been injured or killed? Whereas my pragmatic side argued there'd be no reason to hide the ship.

Gator had seemed determined to keep me from this area. Maybe he'd discovered the ship and toyed with the idea of completing what he'd originally set out to do? But then, he'd decided to give me a chance, and I'd won him over like I hoped? Maybe, like me, he'd fallen under the spell of this place and never wanted to leave? I didn't know.

Taking a seat on a fallen tree trunk, I grew deep in thought. A bunch of little things had happened in the past month that, treated individually, didn't mean too much, but when you added them up, they became significant. Things like how Gator seemed to know exactly where everything in the cabin was located. Extra blankets, dishes, utensils, or cookware we needed, he could easily fish out of the single cupboard or from beneath a narrow wooden counter. He knew where tools were located out back and exactly what was planted in the overgrown garden. Then there was the fact that the only clothes in the cabin seemed to fit him perfectly.

Had I been completely blind? Only seeing what I wanted to see? I leapt to my feet, my hands clenched into fists. There was only one thing to do. I had to confront him.

Something on the ground, sparkling in the sun, caught my eye. I reached down, picked it up, and tucked it in my pocket.

Chapter 9

I stomped into the cabin and slammed the door. Gator was up. He had on his pants and was pulling a shirt over his head.

"We need to talk," I said.

"Good morning to you, too," he said with a lazy smile. "What's so urgent?"

I stared at him a moment, debating what to do, not sure if I wanted to risk it all. If I pissed him off, he might decide to swap me for Mila after all.

"I wanted to get some of that fruit

for breakfast," I began, watching his face for any reaction. *Nothing.*

"I guess you didn't find any?" He looked pointedly at my empty hands.

"I found something else."

His eyebrow rose. "Really?"

Perhaps it was just my imagination, but I thought I detected a glimmer of discomfort in his suddenly shifty gaze. "Yeah. I found a ship covered over by branches like someone was hiding it."

He went and sat down at the table, his eyes avoiding me. "And you're telling me this because you're so anxious to leave all of a sudden?" For some reason, he seemed hurt.

"I'm wondering if you knew it was there."

He shrugged. "What if I did?"

"I'm also wondering about some other stuff. Like about how we just happened to find this so-called abandoned cabin."

"You were there when it happened. We crashed and wandered and came upon it just like that."

"Yeah, just like that. A little convenient, wouldn't you say?"

Now he did look at me. His gaze narrowed. "What? Do you think I planned to crash and keep you here in this cabin with me?" Sweat glistened on his brow.

"I don't know. You tell me."

Shaking his head in denial, he laughed. "That's some plan. You must think I'm something else to go to all this trouble." He glared at me when I remained silent. "If there is a ship, then maybe we should leave like I planned? Considering you suddenly think I'm some master schemer bent on keeping you here against your will." He got to his feet and grabbed the duffle bag, tossing it onto the bed. "Let's go. You're anxious to head to Balenzie and meet the gang. Come to think of it, I miss Mila. A lot less drama."

So, he'd called my bluff, but I didn't believe him. "Spare me the theatrics. You don't plan on going anywhere." He was a better actor than I was.

He strode over and stood before me, chest heaving. I took a step back and reached into my pocket. I pulled out the object I'd found by the ship and held it up before his face. He stared at the small, polished crystal that pulsed with light.

"I poked around some more and found a small mine close by the ship, camouflaged as well. It was full of these," I informed him. "This one was beside the ship." I tossed the crystal to the floor.

He stared into my eyes. When he reached out to take my hand, I backed away.

"I want you to take me home. Now," I insisted.

"But you wanted to stay. You said you did."

"That's before I figured out what a liar you are. It's your ship. This is your planet. Your cabin. It was all a lie."

"I was alone," he whispered. "Everyone's leaving. My planet is dying. I couldn't just abandon it. I tried living on Earth. It was so hard."

He looked so pathetic I almost felt sorry for him—almost. "I don't care. If you try to make me stay here, I will hate you. You can make me do a lot of things, but you can never make me love you. If you want to swap me for Mila, then go ahead."

He stared at me for a long time. "There is no Mila." His voice was barely a whisper.

"What?"

"It was a lie. You're right. I lied about everything. Even her."

I stared at him incredulously. "So you figured I'd be desperate enough to do anything to change your mind about swapping me. Desperate enough to live out the rest of my life here on your dying, sinking planet. Unless that was a lie too."

"No. It is sinking. I was going to tell you the truth. As soon as I was certain you wouldn't leave me." He began to pace, only pausing long enough to bang his fist against the table in anger. "Damn it. I didn't know what else to do. I know you won't believe this, but I'm in love with you. I'm sorry. I hoped you were beginning to love me too."

There were tears in his eyes, but I ignored them. I stomped outside and slammed the door. Several minutes later, he joined me. In silence, we headed toward the orchard.

* * * *

Gator took me home. It took less time than I thought it would. As the ship hovered over my garden late at night, I got up from my seat to leave. He grabbed hold of my hand and stared into my eyes. I glared at him and pulled away.

"Flora," he called after opening the door and allowing me to leave.

I turned back to look at him standing there all alone in the doorway. "Thanks for the ride," I said, then turned and walked away.

Moments later, I heard a slight hum as his ship lifted up and flew off into the sky. I watched it until it disappeared from view, wondering if he'd return to the cabin on his planet or make another attempt to build a life for himself here on Earth. With a great sigh, I went inside my house, allowing my tears to flow.

Though I'd been gone for over a

month, everything appeared the same as I had left it, as if time had frozen in place. However, there were over a hundred messages on my phone, most of which were from my frantic manager. I allowed them to play in the background while I strolled around the house, reacquainting myself with the vast space. Tomorrow would be soon enough to brave opening my email and returning phone calls.

My footsteps echoed as I clumped on lead feet into the kitchen. Dishes sat, washed and dried at the side of the sink, where my housekeeper had left them. There was a nasty little note on the dining room table from her as well, thanking me for checking out without paying her.

I'd noticed the grass in the yard was extra tall, so I assumed my gardener had left me as well. At least I still had electricity and water. Stacks of mail were piled up in front of the mail slot inside my front door, many of them stamped *Past Due*. The stillness and quiet felt suffocating. I stood, staring at the front door, an avalanche of mail before it, almost as though it were keeping everyone out. I half-expected Gator to come exploding inside, busting through the heavy wood, scattering the paper mountain, and rushing to take me into his arms.

And then what? the little voice of reason inside my head demanded. I had no answers.

Later, I sat and soaked in a giant bubble bath. Leaning my head back against my little pink blow-up pillow, I reached for the glass of red wine sitting on the edge of the tub. The half-empty bottle sat on the floor within arm's reach. I had a feeling it was going to take a lot more than alcohol to get through this night.

Tomorrow would be better, I told myself. Soon, the image of Gator's handsome face would fade from my mind, and the sound of his voice and laughter would be nothing but a vague, distasteful memory. And yet, I had to admit, if only to myself, that our time together hadn't been all bad. Despite the lies. Despite the deceit.

I reached for the wine bottle and topped off my glass. Yeah, it was going to be a long night.

Chapter 10

The next morning, I got down to business, getting my life back in order. I couldn't bear to think about Gator. He'd broken my heart with his lies. The fact that he'd gone to such lengths to keep me with him was irrelevant. I could have been any vulnerable female.

I returned phone calls, answered emails, paid bills, and sent out apology notes with checks attached, begging my disgruntled staff to come back to me. I also went on that website that'd started all this nasty business and anonymously added the testament of my encounter. Seeing that all of the other comments consisted of rave reviews—which I'd been naive enough to believe and which I now knew to be fake—I was certain my comment would be quickly deleted. However, if I could save even one person, I'd be satisfied.

I had to come up with a cover story for my manager to tell the media—the truth, of course, being too inconceivable. The most believable thing we decided upon was saying that I'd been in recovery from alcoholism. I actually fed her a BS line about feeling overwhelmed and having to leave town for a while to 'find myself.' Everyone bought our lie, and just like that, I was once again the darling of Hollywood.

Days turned into a week, then two. Nights were the worst. I'd awake often, feeling restless, my body craving Gator's hands and lips. I missed the sound of his deep, even breaths when he slept. The way he reached out for me and pulled me tight against him. The way he was perpetually aroused. How his lips would kiss down the length of my body, lingering on my breasts and between my thighs. The feel of his fingers buried deep inside me while he laved my secret place with his tongue. How the thick fullness of his erection, thrusting deep inside, made me gasp in delight.

Every single hour of every single day passed painfully slow. I tried to throw myself into a new role I'd been offered, but suddenly acting didn't appeal to me. Not since I'd spent a month with the best actor in the galaxy, one who'd played his part to a T. What a joke it was on me that, at the time, I'd thought I had been the one playing him.

After another week, my anger

began to diminish. The good moments I'd spent with Gator came to mind much more than the bad. When I laid in bed at night, my body still ached for his touch. I wondered if I'd ever get past that feeling. I longed for him so much that I cried more than I smiled.

Then one night, I stood in my garden alone, looking up at the full moon in the sky. A tiny light caught my eye, and I watched in fascination as it began to fly closer and closer. Seconds later, a small spacecraft hovered several feet away from me. Warily, I began to creep closer, brushing off my hands and keeping a watchful eye.

The ship's doorway opened, and a large being began to descend. I quickly realized it was Gator. He wasn't alone. Another alien exited the ship and stood beside him. Gathering my courage, I went over, directly into their line of sight. Gator and I locked eyes. All of the moments we had spent together rushed through my mind. I suddenly no longer cared about anything except being in his arms.

"Gator?" My voice sounded like a croak.

"Flora, I miss you," he said.

"I miss you too."

The alien gazed at Gator, then me. "It is done then."

"Yes," Gator said. "It's done."

I had no idea what they meant, but I was beginning to get an uneasy feeling.

The alien nodded its large head and waved around its giant hands. "Three years," it reminded him, then headed back up the stairs into its ship and zoomed away.

It all clicked into place. "No! You can't," I yelled at the retreating ship, then turned my fearful eyes on Gator. What had he done?

He came up before me and took me into his arms. They felt so good around me.

"You made a deal with them? Why didn't you just fly here yourself?"

"I owed you this much," he admitted. "If you didn't want me, then I deserved whatever fate I had coming to me."

I sighed and snuggled closer to him. "They'll come back for you, you know."

He reached into his pocket and pulled out a handful of pulsing crystals. "I brought these along, just in case you let me stay. I'll be ready for them."

I smiled. "So what about your home?"

He held my arms and stepped back to stare into my eyes. "I'm willing to give it up so we can be together. On your terms."

"It's not so great," I admitted, waving my hand around, indicating the life I led. Then a glorious thought entered my mind. "You said you had a cabin on Earth. Was that true?"

He cringed. "Yes, that part was the truth."

I didn't need to think overly long about what I wanted, what mattered to me most. It wasn't the glitz and glamor. It was this man before me, warts and all. "Why don't we go there?"

A large grin replaced his look of disbelief. "I'd love to."

I took his hand. "Okay, help me pack. I'll show you my giant, lonely house."

Laughing, he allowed me to lead him away. As we walked through the garden, we passed a metal garbage can lid lying on the ground. I kicked the small transistor radio that sat beside it into the brush.

When Gator looked quizzically in that direction, I distracted him with a kiss.

I'd been ready to bargain with the alien to gain my desire. I had nearly risked my future freedom, but not for the sake of glitz and glamour—not this time. This time, it'd been for love. I was taking a chance on a future with Gator. Hopefully, he'd learned his lesson about using deception to obtain what he wanted. I know I'd learned my lesson the hard way.

We both craved something the other wished to give freely, without tricks, or bargains, or threats. We both wanted love. And staring up into the handsome face of the man beside me, I knew we'd found it.

Juliet is an award-winning author of several best-selling novels and short stories. She lives in Ontario with her husband, cat and dog. You can check out Juliet's website to see what she's been up to.

http://JulietCardinWebsite.Yolasite.com

www.ingramcontent.com/pod-product-compliance
Lightning Source LLC
La Vergne TN
LVHW090614110826
845146LV00001B/386

* 9 7 9 8 8 9 1 2 6 0 0 2 3 *